NORTH HOFFMAN

DANGER! ACTION! TROUBLE! ADVENTURE!

THE DATA SET

The Sky Is Falling

By Ada Hopper   Illustrated by Sam Ricks

New York

LITTLE SIMON
An imprint of Simon & Schuster Children's Publishing Division
1230 Avenue of the Americas, New York, New York 10020
First Little Simon paperback edition May 2016 • Copyright © 2016 by Simon & Schuster, Inc. All rights reserved, including the right of reproduction in whole or in part in any form. LITTLE SIMON is a registered trademark of Simon & Schuster, Inc., and associated colophon is a trademark of Simon & Schuster, Inc. For information about special discounts for bulk purchases, please contact Simon & Schuster Special Sales at 1-866-506-1949 or business@simonandschuster.com. The Simon & Schuster Speakers Bureau can bring authors to your live event. For more information or to book an event contact the Simon & Schuster Speakers Bureau at 1-866-248-3049 or visit our website at www.simonspeakers.com.
Designed by John Daly. The text of this book was set in Serifa.
Manufactured in the United States of America 0416 FFG 10 9 8 7 6 5 4 3 2 1
Library of Congress Cataloging-in-Publication Data
Names: Hopper, Ada, author. | Ricks, Sam, illustrator. Title: The sky is falling / by Ada Hopper ; illustrated by Sam Ricks. Description: First Little Simon paperback edition. | New York : Little Simon, 2016. | Series: The DATA Set ; #3 | Summary: When Dr. Bunsen's newest invention brings extraterrestrials down to Earth, can second-graders Gabriel, Laura, and Caesar, aka the DATA, keep their town from being space invaded? Identifiers: LCCN 2015027303| ISBN 9781481463102 (hardback) | ISBN 9781481463096 (pbk) | ISBN 9781481463119 (ebook) Subjects: | CYAC: Inventions—Fiction. | Extraterrestrial beings—Fiction. | Clubs—Fiction. | Adventure and adventurers—Fiction. | BISAC: JUVENILE FICTION / Readers / Chapter Books. | JUVENILE FICTION / Adventure and adventurers—Fiction. | JUVENILE FICTION / Science Fiction. Classification: LCC PZ7.1.H66 Sk 2016 | DDC [Fic]—dc23
LC record available at http://lccn.loc.gov/2015027303

CONTENTS

Chapter 1

Earth to Laura

It was a bright and early Monday morning in Newtonburg. The sun was shining. The birds were chirping. Rush-hour traffic was backing up. The start to a perfectly ordinary day.

Except it wasn't.

"Where in the world is Laura?"

Gabe and Cesar pedaled their bikes at top speed. "We're going to be late!"

They ditched their bikes in Gabe's driveway and raced to the backyard. Normally, the three friends known as the DATA Set (Danger! Action! Trouble!

Adventure!) would already be on their way to school. But Laura hadn't shown up at the corner as usual. Something was up.

Gabe and Cesar used the pulley elevator to get to the top of the DATA Set's super-awesome tree house.

Sure enough, they found Laura inside, busy at work on an invention. She was so focused, she didn't even hear them come in.

"Earth to Laura!" Gabe called.

She jumped. "Oh, hey, guys. Sorry. When I'm in the zone, it's like I'm on another planet. What time is it?" She looked at her watch. "Whoa!"

"I know," said Gabe. "We're going to have to pedal at least"—he did a quick calculation—"two point six times faster than normal to make it to school on time."

"Here, my mom sent us the perfect 'on-the-go' breakfast." Cesar passed each of his friends a bagel. "What are you working on?"

"Cesar, we don't have time . . ."

But Gabe was too late. Laura's eyes lit up. She couldn't resist showing off her latest invention. "Check it out!" she exclaimed.

On a table was a large metal box with lots of knobs and speakers. It had an oversize antenna that poked straight through the roof of the tree house.

"Is it a toaster?" Cesar asked curiously.

"No." Laura frowned. "Does it look like a toaster?"

"No. But a toaster would make my bagel tastier. And toastier."

Laura giggled. "Well, I can't help your bagel. But I can help if you want to listen to someone in Russia. I built an international

radio! This antenna can pick up signals halfway around the world."

She adjusted the knobs. The radio made high-pitched whines and squeaks. Suddenly, a Russian man's voice echoed from the speakers!

"Pretty cool, huh?" she said proudly.

"They make Russian bagels, you know." Cesar munched. "Pumpernickel bread with seeds. They're better toasted."

Gabe and Laura shook their heads.

Suddenly, the Russian man's voice fizzled out. It was replaced by

loud, repeating buzzes and beeps.

Bzzz. Bzz-bzz. Beep-boop-beep!

"What happened?" asked Gabe.

Laura shrugged. "I'm not sure."

"Maybe we can help you fix it,"
said Gabe. "After school, that is.

Come on, DATA Set. Trouble may be in our name, but if there's one person I don't want to be in trouble with, it's Principal Stevens!"

Chapter 2

Alien Alert

"You three are in serious trouble!"

Principal Stevens loomed over Gabe, Laura, and Cesar.

"But we're not late yet!" Laura protested. "The bell won't ring for"—she checked the clock—"two minutes and thirty-two seconds . . . thirty-one seconds . . . thirty . . ."

"Did we do something wrong?" asked Gabe.

Principal Stevens looked very serious. "I'm afraid so. It seems you three have been selected for . . ." He broke out in a big grin. "The State Regional Science Challenge! Congratulations, DATA Set! Your hydroelectricity project was

chosen to represent our school!"

"Phew." Gabe, Laura, and Cesar breathed sighs of relief. Principal Stevens had a way of pulling tricks like that.

"That's awesome!" said Gabe.

"Wait until we tell our parents. And Dr. Bunsen."

"He helped us with the design," Laura explained.

Principal Stevens adjusted his glasses. "Oh, yes, I do remember Dr. Bunsen being at the science day." He paused. "Strange fellow. Kept talking to me about the molecular properties of mung beans."

He stared into space for a second. "Anyway, I'll let you kids get to class so you're not actually in trouble. Congratulations again. Oh, and watch out for aliens!"

The principal whistled a tune as he walked away.

"Have you guys noticed that all the adults in our lives are weird?" Cesar asked.

"What do you think he meant by 'aliens'?" Laura said as they

walked to class. "Did we miss something?"

"I guess we'll have to wait and find out," said Gabe.

Luckily for the three friends, they didn't have to wait long.

"Guys, did you *see* them last

night?" A boy named Cole eagerly hurried up to the DATA Set.

"See what?" asked Gabe. He looked around the classroom. Kids were chattering more excitedly than usual.

"The *lights*," Cole insisted, a wild look in his eyes. "Everyone in town saw the most insane lights in the sky last night! Like laser beams streaking in every direction!"

"My dad said it was probably the aurora borealis." A girl named Heather turned in her chair. "That can happen, you know."

"Or maybe a secret government project," another boy, Chaz, piped up. "My dad said the military is always doing stuff like that. That's why he wants to move off the grid."

"Nah," said Cole. "I'll tell you what it was. *Aliens.* Definitely UFOs. Guys—it's happening. Proof of extraterrestrial life!"

But Gabe, Cesar, and Laura had another idea. Whenever something strange or mysterious happened in Newtonburg, it tended to be the work of one man. He could be a little spacey. But he was definitely not an alien.

And his name started with a *B*.

Chapter 3

The Bunsimmunicator 3000

"Why, of course it was me!"

Dr. Bunsen scurried around his lab collecting odds and ends while the DATA Set watched.

"But what were the lights for?" Gabe asked. "The whole town thinks they were from UFOs."

"From, no. To, yes!" The doctor

disappeared into another room carrying a huge pile of supplies.

Gabe looked at his friends. They shrugged. The DATA Set had known Dr. Bunsen for a while now. But sometimes he could still be very confusing.

Laura hopped up on a lab stool. "Mind telling us what's up?"

"Ah, yes, of course." The doctor

emerged and dusted his hands on his lab coat. "You see, I've invented a device that communicates with both light *and* radio waves. The Bunsimmunicator 3000!"

The kids followed Dr. Bunsen to a large

control screen. It operated an enormous satellite dish attached to the mansion's roof.

"The Bunsimmunicator 3000 has been sending the same message in light and radio waves into deep space for the past twenty-four hours," the doctor explained.

"But why?" Cesar asked, chewing a granola bar.

"To communicate with aliens, my dear always-hungry boy!"

Suddenly, a timer went off at the other corner of the lab.

"Whoops!" The doctor hurried away.

Laura stepped closer to the controls. "Wow," she breathed. "Do you think it could actually work?"

"What's the message saying?" Gabe asked.

"Bunsen code!" the doctor called from inside a closet. "Or I should

say, a guide for communicating in Bunsen code." He came out wearing a white zip-up suit. "I developed a simple language based on tones and rhythms to project into space."

"You mean like Morse code?" Laura asked.

"Better!" the doctor exclaimed. "My hope is that aliens can use it to communicate with us. The Bunsimmunicator 3000 will send that message into space for the next ten years."

"Ten years!" exclaimed the friends.

"But the lights freaked out the entire town in just one night," said Gabe.

"Oh." The doctor looked at the control screen. "Well, I suppose I could adjust the machine to send the light portion only during the daytime, when it's not visible."

Suddenly, the doctor picked up a crazy-looking helmet covered in wires.

"Now, then, I'm afraid that I'm scheduled to begin yet another experiment in precisely"—he looked at the timer—"now. Will you three be all right without me for the next few days?"

"I guess so," said Cesar. "But what happens if, say, something responds to your . . . Bun-si-mu-ni-cator 3000?" he asked, reading the

name on the control screen. "Can we come get you?"

The doctor waved his hand. "No need to worry. It would take months for an alien to learn the code. Years, perhaps. My new experiment will be quite complete by then!"

"Okay," Gabe said. "As long as you're sure."

Chapter 4

We Are Coming

Two days later, the friends were doing homework in the tree house after school. Laura had her radio tuned to the frequency of Dr. Bunsen's message.

Bzzz. Bzz-bzz. Beep-boop-beep!

It turned out, that was the buzzing and beeping they'd heard on Monday. The friends had been listening to it on repeat for so long, they didn't even notice it in the background anymore.

"I think it would be cool if aliens had eight arms." Cesar doodled a sketch of an alien on his homework. "Can you imagine the juggling skills?"

"How about ten legs?" Gabe chimed in. "With a propeller tail so it could run superfast."

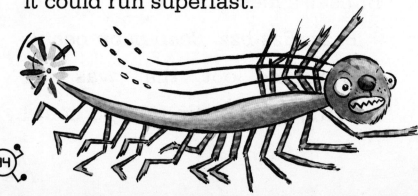

"Or two brains!" Cesar exclaimed.

Gabe shook his head. "Wouldn't the two brains compete with each other?"

"That's why it'd have eight arms," Cesar said. "To duke it out with itself!"

Cesar pretended to battle with himself like a double-brained alien. Laura and Gabe laughed.

"I think any alien we'd meet would be super-intelligent," said Laura. "It would have to be, because it would have figured out intergalactic space travel. And Dr. Bunsen's message."

"I'd like to meet an alien," Gabe said thoughtfully. "As long as it was friendly. Guys, imagine if aliens were watching us on Earth right now. Just waiting for the right time to reach out and . . ."

Suddenly, Laura's radio began making high-pitched whines and squeaks again. Static fizzled from the speakers, and then . . .

Boop! Boop!
Bzz-bzz-bzz!

Slowly, the friends looked at the radio.

"Laura, did you do that?" Gabe asked.

"No," said Laura. "Maybe Dr. B. changed the pattern. Or maybe . . ."

Quickly, they grabbed Dr. B.'s

Bunsen code manual to translate the message. He'd given them a copy to hold on to while he was busy with his other experiment.

"What does it say, Laura?" Cesar

asked anxiously. "Can you make sense of those weird sounds?"

"Hang on," Laura said. "Okay, that first sound"—the friends listened to the *boop*—"means 'We.' And the next part means 'are.' And that last sound . . ." Laura trailed off.

"What?" cried Gabe and Cesar.

Laura stared at the page, eyes wide.

"Coming," she said quietly. "It means, 'We are coming.'"

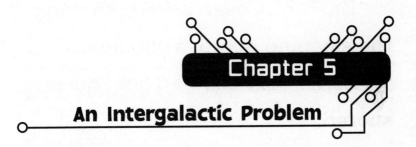

Chapter 5

An Intergalactic Problem

"Dr. B.! Dr. B.!"

Gabe, Laura, and Cesar sprinted into Dr. Bunsen's mansion. But his lab was eerily quiet.

"Where is he?" Gabe asked.

"Maybe in that side room?" Laura pointed.

The friends hurried inside. Sure

enough, there was Dr. Bunsen.

But he was sound asleep!

"Dr. B.?" Cesar asked, shaking the sleeping doctor's shoulder.

"Zzzzzzzzzzzz." The doctor snored.

Dr. Bunsen was seated in a reclining chair wearing the electrode helmet. He was hooked up to various tubes through the special white zip-up suit the kids had seen him put on the other day.

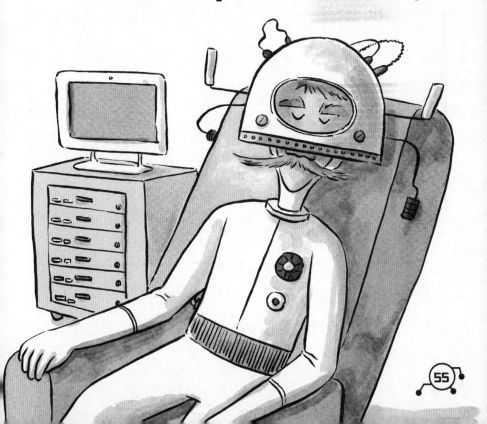

"Is he okay?" Laura asked.

"Greetings!"

A computer screen suddenly lit up, projecting an image of the doctor. "This is a prerecorded

message. If you are seeing this, it means you have visited while I am in the midst of my Ultrasonic Dream-o-rama experiment. Never fear! I will be awake again on Friday morning. In the meantime, please help yourself to king-size chocolate bars with extra nuts!"

An automatic drawer opened, revealing a box of chocolate the DATA Set had sold Dr. Bunsen when they'd first met him.

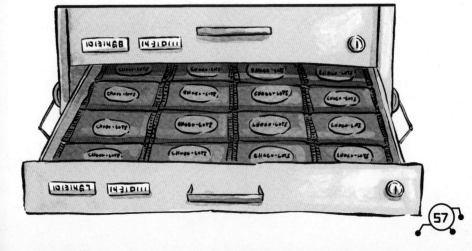

"I don't believe this," said Gabe.

"What are we going to do?" asked Laura.

"Holy molars! He still *has* those?" Cesar stared in disbelief at the chocolate. "I thought he said he liked chocolate!"

"Come on, Cesar, focus," said Gabe. "There are aliens on their way to Earth, and the guy who called them is sleeping for the next two days."

"We need to go back to the tree house," said Laura. "Maybe we can figure out a way to send a message using Dr. B.'s manual, telling the aliens *not* to come."

"Like, 'Thanks, but no thanks'?" asked Gabe.

"Something like that," said Laura.

Cesar picked up several chocolate bars. "Well, he said 'help yourself.' And I know *I* like chocolate."

Quickly, the friends left. But they bumped into their classmate Cole on the way back to their tree house.

"Guys, did you see that just now?" Cole stopped his bike. "The lights. They're back!"

"They are?" Laura asked. She whispered to Gabe and Cesar, "But we were just at Dr. B.'s, and the light-wave signal wasn't on."

Cole was ecstatic. "It was different this time! The light came from the sky down to Earth! I'm going to get my camera. Something *big* is going on."

Gabe, Laura, and Cesar watched
him go.

"This doesn't sound good," said
Gabe. "I hope we're not too late."

They took the elevator into the tree house. But just as Laura ran inside, she noticed that something was different. "Guys, did you move my radio?"

Gabe and Cesar looked over to the corner of the tree house.

There was the radio on its side. It looked like someone

had changed the radio station too.
The DATA Set heard something
move at the other end of the room.
That was when they realized that
they were not alone.

Chapter 6

Laura's Alien Best Friend

"Bzzz voop beep zoop?"

The DATA Set was in shock—there was an alien in their tree house, and it was trying to communicate with them in Bunsen code!

"Uh, guys, what do we do?" Cesar asked.

The friends stared at the alien. It blinked its enormous black eyes.

"Does it look friendly to you?" asked Gabe.

"Maybe," said Laura. "Let's try to talk to it." She reached for the Bunsen code manual.

"Bzzz bzzz bzzz!" The alien backed away.

"It's okay, it's okay," Laura said calmly. "I just need to grab this."

The alien watched Laura curiously. It wasn't much smaller than she was. But it had an oversized head, had smooth gray skin and long, skinny fingers on each of its four arms.

Laura flipped through the manual. "I can't be sure, but I think it's asking for help."

"Bzzz voop beep boom."

"Stand by." Laura scanned the manual. "Something about 'call' and 'crash.'"

"Do you think it crash-landed its spaceship?" Cesar asked.

"That could have been the light Cole saw," said Gabe.

"And 'call' could be about my radio," Laura said. "The signal coming from it is pretty strong. Maybe it thinks this is where Dr. B.'s message came from."

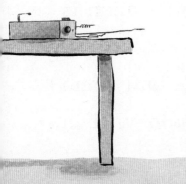

The alien tilted its head and blinked.

"This is going to sound weird," said Cesar. "But the little alien is kind of cute."

"Well, then, there's only one thing to do," Gabe said with a confident grin. "We're the DATA Set, and the alien needs help. So it's our job to keep it safe until Dr. B. wakes up. Team, we have an intergalactic guest for the next two days!"

Later that night the DATA Set sat in the tree house with the alien. It turned out, Laura had been right: This alien *was* supersmart. Not only had it deciphered Bunsen code, but it had quickly learned to communicate using hand signals, too, which was a whole lot easier.

The alien had even managed to tell them its name: Fave.

Fave studied all the gadgets in the DATA Set's tree house.

"I made them," Laura said proudly, pointing to the inventions, then herself.

The alien reached out and

touched Laura's sleeve.

"Right!" said Laura. "Me."

The alien tapped Laura's radio and then touched her sleeve again.

"Yup," Laura said. "I made that."

"Here, Fave." Cesar offered a piece of chocolate. "You must be hungry!"

The alien sniffed the chocolate. It nibbled it.

"Bzzzzphhhhbleeeeghhh!"

Fave spit it out!

"Not a fan of extra nuts, huh?" asked Cesar.

"Try this." Laura offered Fave a celery stick from her backpack.

Fave gingerly tasted the celery. It liked that a lot!

The alien touched her sleeve again.

"Laura, if I didn't know any better, I'd say you have a new best friend," Gabe said with a smile.

Chapter 7

Unexpected Visitors

The next morning, at school, the friends whispered at their desks.

"I hope Fave will be okay in the tree house all day," Laura said.

"At least there isn't anything in the news about the lights," Gabe whispered. "No one seems to have found Fave's spaceship."

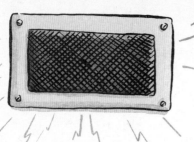

"No one that we know of," Cesar pointed out.

Suddenly, Principal Stevens's voice came over the loudspeaker.

"Will Gabriel, Laura, and Cesar please report to my office?"

"Ooooooooooooh," the class echoed in unison.

"We've never been called down to the principal's office!" exclaimed Cesar. "This can't be good."

A few minutes later, the friends found Principal Stevens waiting for them.

"Is this about the science challenge?" Laura asked hopefully.

The principal shook his head. "I'm afraid not. There are some

men from the government here who would like to speak with you."

Gabe, Laura, and Cesar gulped. Behind Principal Stevens were three men in suits and dark glasses.

"If you'll each follow us," the men said.

"Gabe?" Laura called when she realized they were being led to separate rooms.

"It's okay." Gabe tried not to sound as nervous as he was.

Gabe followed his agent to an office down the hall. The agent

closed the door.

"Do you know this man?" He placed a photograph of Dr. Bunsen on the desk.

"Oh, sure," Gabe said, trying to sound casual. "That's Dr. B."

"And have you ever noticed anything . . . unusual about him?"

"Everything is unusual about him!" Gabe laughed awkwardly.

The agent didn't seem amused. "Tell me more."

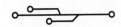

"Of course we know Dr. B.,"
Laura said in the next office over.
"He has helped
us with a few
of our science
projects."

"Yes, yes, we
hear he's quite
the scientist,"
said the agent.
"What else has he invented?"

Laura gulped. "Oh, you know,
standard stuff. Bug zappers. Laser
beams. Maybe a growth ray . . ."

"Then there was this one time we went flying in his Omega moon-p o w e r e d hover car!" Cesar explained excitedly to his agent. "The Midnight Rider 2.0. It happened right after we chased a tornado using his Cyclo-tronic Navigator. Boy, *that* was a *crazy* week!"

After the agents finished questioning the kids, Gabe, Laura, and Cesar were allowed to return to class. They didn't talk about it until the end of the day—with so many students around, who knew where it was safe to talk anymore!

Finally, school let out. The DATA Set raced all the way home to the safety of the tree house.

Fave was there, tinkering with Laura's radio.

"Those guys meant business," said Gabe, out of breath.

"I don't think we can wait for Dr. B." Laura was pretty worked up. "We have to figure out a way to get Fave home now!"

"But it's not like we can fix Fave's spaceship," said Cesar. "Fave was smart enough to decipher Dr. B.'s code, and even we don't know how to do that."

"Dr. B.'s code," Gabe said slowly. "Guys, I think I have a plan."

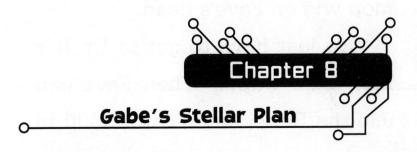

Chapter 8

Gabe's Stellar Plan

"This is never going to work."

Cesar peeked around the corner of the house.

"Seriously. This plan has 'not going to work' written all over it."

Behind him, Gabe and Laura stood on either side of Fave. They had disguised the alien in a white lab coat and goggles. And for extra measure, they'd thrown a brown mop wig on Fave's head.

"We just have to get to Dr. B.'s lab," said Gabe. "Then Fave can use the Bunsimmunicator 3000 to send a message home."

"Fave, I told you not to bring that." Laura tried to wriggle her radio free from the little alien's hands. But Fave stubbornly held on to it with a four-armed, twenty-fingered grip.

Laura sighed. "Fine. Bring it. But let's go."

Quietly, the friends snuck down
from the tree house and around
the corner.

"There you are!"

The DATA Set jumped. It was Cole! He skidded up to them on his bike.

"I've been looking all over for you," Cole said. "I know you're into science and stuff, so you're the perfect team to help me track

down the light from the sky. I'm . . .
Oh, who's that?"

Cole had spotted Fave.

"Haven't you ever met Dr.
Bunsen?" Gabe said, thinking fast.

"I guess not." Cole paused. "I
always pictured him taller. What's
he carrying?"

Cole reached out toward Laura's radio, which Fave was gripping with all four hands!

"Don't!" said Laura. "It's broken. Dr. Bunsen is going to help us fix it."

Cole looked confused. "But what is it?"

"A toaster," Cesar said. "And my bagels won't be kept waiting. Sorry—gotta go."

The friends scurried off, leaving a very suspicious Cole staring after them.

"That was close," said Gabe. "Hopefully we don't bump into anyone—"

"Mi hijo!"

Gabe groaned. His mom was running up to them, carrying his little sister, Juanita.

"Could you drop this in the mail for me, *cariño*?" His mother handed him an envelope. "Juanita has a doctor's appointment, and the post office closes in fifteen minutes."

"Uh, sure, Mom," said Gabe. He

watched in mild horror as Juanita reached out to play with one of Fave's four arms. Fave slowly

pulled its arm back inside the lab coat. Juanita giggled.

"Thank you!" Gabe's mom raced off with Juanita.

Gabe sighed in relief. "Come on.

Let's go before the entire town stops by to say hello."

Moving as stealthily as they could, the friends crept toward Dr. Bunsen's house.

They were almost there, when . . .

"Oh, no," said Cesar. "You guys aren't going to believe this!"

Down the street were the government agents. And Cole was on his bike, pointing them in the DATA Set's direction!

Chapter 9

A Message Home

The government agents walked straight toward the DATA Set. There was nowhere to hide!

"We suspected we might find you three here," the lead agent said. "Where's Dr. Bunsen?"

Gabe, Laura, and Cesar didn't know how to get out of this one!

But before they could respond, Fave raised its hand.

"Dr. Bunsen, eh?" said the agent. He looked Fave up and down. "Strange. From the photo, you seemed . . . taller."

"Dr. B.'s not feeling well," Gabe said hurriedly. "He has a really bad cold."

"We need to get him inside to rest," said Laura.

"Not so fast," said the lead agent. "We need

to have a word with Dr. Bunsen."

Suddenly, Fave sneezed all over them! Great green globs of alien snot goo dripped from the agents' sunglasses onto their shoes.

"It's *really* bad," said Cesar. "Please come back tomorrow!"

With that, the three friends

rushed Fave inside the mansion and slammed the door.

"Phew," said Gabe. "Do you think they'll leave?"

"Let's not wait to find out," said Laura. "Come on—to the Bunsimmunicator 3000!"

They clambered into Dr. B.'s lab. When they reached the Bunsimmunicator 3000, the screen lit up.

Bzzz. Bzz-bzz. Beep-boop-beep!

It was still sending out the Bunsen code on repeat into space.

"Laura, can you program it so

Fave can send a message instead?" Gabe asked.

Laura's fingers flew over the digital keyboard.

"Access denied," the computer said.

"We'll see about that." Laura typed in a few more commands.

"Passcode?" the computer asked.

"Uh-oh," said Laura. "I didn't think it would be password protected. If I can't get in, we can't change the message."

Fave touched Laura's sleeve. It held out her radio.

"I'm sorry, buddy," she said. "But I'm not sure what to . . ."

Laura looked at the radio more closely. Her eyes lit up. "No way! I don't believe it. Fave's modified my radio! Check it out—it has a microphone now. We can hook it up to Dr. B.'s satellite and send a message using *it*!"

"That's why Fave insisted on bringing it," exclaimed Gabe.

Quickly, the friends hooked up Laura's radio to Dr. B.'s satellite controls. Then Fave spoke into the microphone.

"*Guuughghhlggh cluggghhhhdsh favlooooovichhhh.*"

A minute later, the doorbell rang.

"I'll get it," said Cesar, forgetting himself.

"No!" cried Gabe and Laura.

But it was too late. Cesar opened the door.

FWOOSH!

The friends were sucked up in a tractor beam, pulled out the front door . . . and into a UFO!

Chapter 10

Out of This World

The DATA Set and Fave huddled
close together. All around them
was bright, white light.

Suddenly, two familiar, yet odd-
looking figures approached.

"BLEERRRRGHFFFLUGH!"

Fave raced forward and into
the arms of the two other aliens.

The creatures looked just like Fave, except larger.

"What's happening?" Laura whispered to Gabe.

"I don't know," Gabe whispered back.

The aliens looked at the DATA

Set. One of them held up a glowing orange orb.

It spoke, but the friends heard English this time instead of Fave's language. The orb was translating the words!

"Thank you for bringing our son back to us."

"Your son?" Cesar asked in disbelief. "Fave's a kid?"

"Are you its, uh, his parents?" Laura asked.

"Yes," the aliens said through their translator. "Our son heard your message and wanted to visit Earth. We told him 'no,' but he beamed down anyway."

"Beamed down!" said Cesar. "No wonder we couldn't find a spaceship!"

Fave looked sad.

"He is very curious. We are grateful for your help in finding him and keeping him safe. We will send you back to your planet now."

Suddenly, Fave rushed back to the DATA Set. He tugged at Laura's sleeve.

"I think he wants you to come with him," Gabe said.

Laura smiled and shook her head. "I'm sorry, but I can't, Fave. I have a family, too, on Earth."

Fave held her sleeve for a moment longer. Then he handed her back her radio.

"Of course," Laura said. "I promise to keep in touch."

The next afternoon, Gabe, Laura, and Cesar waited for Dr. B. to wake up from his experiment. They couldn't wait to tell him about their alien adventure!

But first they had to warn him about the government agents.

"Maybe he can lie low until this whole thing blows over," said Gabe.

Dr. Bunsen's experiment timer counted down.

Three . . . two . . . one . . .

The doctor woke up with a big yawn!

"Why, hello, my curious DATA Set!" he exclaimed. "I didn't expect to see you here."

Suddenly, the doorbell rang.

"It seems I am quite popular!" cried the doctor.

"No!" the DATA Set warned.

But it was too late. Dr. B. opened the door. The government agents were there!

"Dr. Bunsen?" they asked.

"That is me!" cried the doctor.

"You're a hard man to get ahold of. We have a surprise for you. . . ."

"Dr. B., run!" cried Gabe.

But before anyone could move, the agent whipped out a glass plaque. "We're here to officially present you with the National Invention Achievement Award for your contributions to science!"

"*That's* why you questioned us?" cried Laura, Gabe, and Cesar.

Dr. Bunsen scratched his head in bewildered delight. "What a pleasant surprise."

"You're looking better, too," the lead agent commented. "And . . . 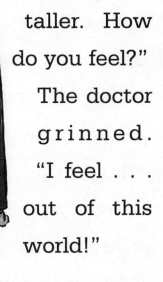 taller. How do you feel?"

The doctor grinned. "I feel . . . out of this world!"

CHECK OUT THE NEXT DATA SET ADVENTURE!

DANGER! ACTION! TROUBLE! ADVENTURE!

THE D.A.T.A SET

Robots Rule the School

By Ada Hopper ○ Illustrated by Sam Ricks

4

Giant robotic planes did loop-the-loops in the sky! Fireworks burst in the air! Mechanical arms clapped and cheered while a little boy hugged a robot puppy.

"Gee, Sprocket," the boy said. "The future is awesome!"

"Arf, arf!" said the robot puppy in

electronic barks.

"That's right, Timmy," said an announcer. "The future *is* awesome. And . . . the future . . . is . . . NOW! . . . now . . . now . . . now. . . ."

The announcer's voice faded out as Gabe, Laura, and Cesar's science teacher, Mrs. Bell, turned off the Smart Board.

"And that," said Mrs. Bell, "leads us into our chapter on robotics." She began passing out assignment packets. "Your assignment this week is to invent your own robots!"

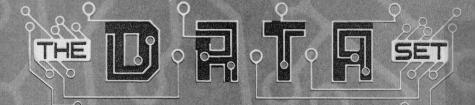

THE DATA SET